⋆⋆ VERA VANCE ⋆⋆

COMICS STAR

Claudia Mills

pictures by Grace Zong

SCHOLASTIC INC.

★

For Jeannie Mobley,
with thanks for the joy of writing
in your sunroom together

★

Text copyright © 2020 by Claudia Mills.

Illustrations copyright © 2020 by Grace Zong.

All rights reserved. Published by Scholastic Inc., 557 Broadway, New York, NY 10012, by arrangement Holiday House Publishing, Inc.

Printed in the U.S.A.

ISBN 978-1-338-85666-8

4 5 6 7 8 9 10   40   31 30 29 28 27 26 25 24 23

Scholastic Inc., 557 Broadway, New York, NY 10012

★ one ★

BAM! *BOOM! KAPOW!*

Vera Vance let go of her bowling ball, hoping this time to hear ten pins exploding into the air. But her ball rolled so slowly and crookedly down the lane again that only one pin, on the far left, wobbled for a second before toppling over.

"Hooray!" Nixie Ness shouted, pumping her fist.

Vera didn't have a lot of friends yet. She and her mother had moved to Longwood for her mother's new job right before school began two months ago. But she and Nixie had just finished being in an after-school cooking camp together, and now Nixie had invited her to come bowling on Saturday afternoon.

Vera stared at Nixie. "Hooray?"

"You got a point! Your first point!"

"You're starting to figure it out," Nixie's father chimed in, sounding almost as enthusiastic as Nixie herself.

Vera couldn't help laughing. So far the only thing she had figured out in her first time ever bowling was that she was terrible at it. Nixie was almost as bad at bowling as Vera. The difference between Vera and Nixie was that when Nixie knocked down a single pin, she started talking about how she was going to be the third-grade bowling champion of the world. Vera just saw the other nine pins still standing.

"Roll again," Nixie's father told her. "You have another roll coming to you."

This time, to Vera's astonishment, four more pins went down.

"See!" Nixie squealed. "Didn't I tell you you'd be great at bowling?"

Vera felt herself beaming. She could imagine drawing a comic of the bowling pins flying into the air with surprised expressions on their faces. All Vera could think about these days was making comics: on Monday, the After-School Superstars program she and Nixie attended was starting a four-week comic-book camp.

As Nixie readied herself for her next turn, Vera wondered whether the bowling pins should look sad instead of surprised when they got smashed by the bowling ball. It was hard not to feel sorry for the poor bowling pins, standing up straight and proud one moment, then clobbered the next.

No, Vera decided. Right this minute— bowling with Nixie and looking forward to comic-book camp together—she wasn't going to think sad thoughts about anything.

☆ ☆ ☆

The next day, Nixie came over to Vera's house after lunch. They had never had a play-date before, and now they were having two in the same weekend. Once Nixie's family had invited Vera to go bowling, Vera's mother had immediately issued an invitation of their own to Nixie. She called it "reciprocating." Vera knew her mother liked to get "reciprocating" over with as soon as possible.

"What do you want to do?" Vera asked as soon as her mother had welcomed Nixie and then tactfully disappeared into the home office where she did stuff for her job as a financial planner.

"I don't know. What do you want to do?" Nixie replied.

Vera felt a twinge of nervousness. It was easier to go bowling with a friend because then it was obvious what you were supposed to do: bowl! For an at-home playdate you were supposed to play. But what if the other person didn't like playing the same things you did?

"I know!" Nixie said. Vera relaxed. "Show me your room! Didn't you tell me you were making a comic book about animals? I love animals! Well, dogs mainly. Not cats. But if there are cats in your book, that's okay, too."

Half an hour later the girls were lying on Vera's neatly made bed, side by side, drawing dogs. Vera's dogs looked more like dogs than Nixie's did, because Vera borrowed details from her big animal encyclopedia, while Nixie just made them up out of her head. But Nixie was great at thinking of funny things for the dogs to be doing and saying.

"How about they go to a doggie school?"

Nixie suggested. "Like maybe it's called Bow-Wow Elementary."

Vera thought for a moment. "Or Mistress Barker's Bow-Wow Academy."

"Yes! That's perfect!" Nixie shouted. "What street should it be on?"

The answer came to Vera instantly. "Wag-a-Tail Lane."

Nixie tossed a fistful of colored pencils into the air in clear appreciation of Vera's brilliance. The pencils clattered onto the hardwood floor.

Just then Vera's mother poked her head into the room. "It sounds like you two are having fun," she said.

"Are we making too much noise?" Vera asked.

"No, not at all," her mother said. "Well, maybe a tiny bit." She smiled when she said it. Vera knew her mother wanted her to have friends in Longwood as much as she did.

"Vera is a great draw-er," Nixie said.

"Nixie is a terrific artist, too," Vera said in return.

Nixie's face lit up. "If we get to have partners in comic-book camp, let's work together.

Our comic book will totally be the best! We could make a whole Bow-Wow Academy comic, with the dogs as superheroes, each one with a different superpower. Not just superbarking, or superbiting, or super-peeing-on-fire-hydrants, but really cool superpowers, like turning into other animals—like maybe one dog turns into an elephant and can spray water from her trunk to put out fires!"

If they had to have comic-book partners, of course Vera wanted Nixie for hers. But part of Vera hoped they'd get to work alone. What if she and Nixie disagreed on ideas? So far they had agreed on everything about Mistress Barker's Bow-Wow Academy. But in the space of a minute Nixie had already gone ahead and practically planned out the whole book.

Before Vera could think of how to reply to Nixie, her mother said, "I'm not sure Vera's doing the comic-book camp."

No! Not that again! Vera's mother had been talking about hiring a sitter to drive Vera to some other enrichment activity instead, like the kids' Science Discovery class at the university. She always told Vera comics weren't "real literature," but Vera devoured comics and graphic novels in the library at school. She loved everything about them—the way she could be swept along in the story by the words *and* the pictures and feel like she was right there having adventures side by side with kids so much braver than she could ever be.

The camp was starting tomorrow! Her mother couldn't change her mind about it one day before the most wonderful camp in the world was going to begin.

Could she?

Nixie opened her mouth as if she was about to explain to Mrs. Vance how Vera *had* to be in the comic-book camp, she just *had* to. But then Nixie's mouth closed again. It was clear Vera's mother wasn't someone who could be told what she *had* to do.

"I want to go to the comic-book camp," Vera said in a small voice.

"I know you do," her mom replied. "But why would a school *enrichment* program devote an entire camp to *comic* books when there are so many other truly important things in the world to learn about?"

Vera stared down silently at the dog pictures she and Nixie had drawn. If only Nixie hadn't mentioned dogs peeing on fire hydrants! That was exactly the kind of thing her mother didn't like.

Her mother sighed. "Honey, I'm willing to give the comic-book camp a try for now. But if you're bored because it's not challenging enough, we can make whatever changes in your schedule we need to. All right, girls, I'll let you go back to your fun."

Vera's mother gave both girls a smile before heading downstairs again.

After a moment of silence, Nixie said, "She did say you could do the camp."

"She said I could do it *for now*."

"Can you talk to your dad?"

Vera took a deep breath. "I don't have a dad. He died in a car accident when I was two."

Nixie's face crumpled. "I shouldn't have . . . I mean . . . I didn't know. I'm sorry, Vera."

"That's okay." Vera was used to answering questions about her dad in a matter-of-fact voice without making the other person feel bad for having asked. But this time her voice had come out shakier than usual. "Well, let's draw some more."

"I'm tired of drawing."

Vera knew Nixie hadn't been the tiniest bit tired of drawing before her mother had come into the room.

"I have an idea!" Nixie said. "Let's look at animal pictures in your encyclopedia and each pick out the top ten animals we'd adopt if our parents let us have pets."

"Okay," Vera agreed.

But she didn't care if her mother might someday let her have a dog, or an elephant, or a pygmy three-toed sloth. She only cared whether her mother would let her keep going to comic-book camp after school every single day for a whole entire month.

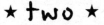

two

The first thing Vera noticed when she and Nixie came into the Longwood Elementary School library on Monday afternoon with the rest of the third-grade after-school comic-book campers was that both comic-book camp teachers had tattoos.

Big tattoos.

Bright tattoos.

Lots of tattoos. Covering their arms and what she could see of their legs, as if they were walking, talking comic books themselves.

Vera felt a prickle of worry. What if her mother saw these teachers and their big, bright tattoos? Vera's mother did not approve of tattoos. By tomorrow, Vera could be whisked off to a science class instead.

Colleen, the head camp lady, checked everyone in on her attendance sheet. Colleen had run the cooking camp, too. She wasn't a cook or a comic-book artist herself; she was the person who kept everything and everybody organized and orderly. It was comforting to see her taking charge again here.

"Grab a snack and sit anywhere," Colleen told them.

Vera and Nixie found seats at a table near the window next to Nolan Nanda and Boogie Bass, who had been their cooking teammates at the last camp. Nolan was serious like Vera and full of fascinating facts about everything. He was already telling Boogie that Superman was invented by two high-school kids who sold their idea to a big comics company for only $130. Boogie was the opposite of serious—funny in a klutzy, good-natured way.

"All right, campers," Colleen said, once everyone was seated at a library table. "I'd like to introduce our comic-book teachers, Brian and Bee. They've collaborated on fifteen comic books and right now they're making a new one for kids about . . . yes . . . how to make comic books! Can you give them your best After-School Superstars welcome?"

Vera joined in the enthusiastic applause, and the two comic-book teachers each waved a tattooed arm and smiled.

Brian had a thin gray ponytail hanging halfway down his back. Bee's hair was short: green-tinted spikes like newly mown grass growing out of her head.

Vera's fingers itched to try drawing Bee. What would be a good name for Bee if she was a comic-book character? Maybe Buzz-Bee. Was it mean to give someone a comic-book name and draw her head looking like a bowling ball with grass sprouting on top? Probably not, Vera concluded. Not in a comic-book camp.

Brian spoke first. "We could start by telling you the long history of blah-blah-blah, and the seven most important rules for blah-blah-blah, then *more* stuff about comic-book blah-blah-blah, or we could jump right in and draw a bunch of cool stuff. Who wants to draw?"

The other fifteen campers cheered their

approval. Vera must have been the only one who wanted to know: Well, how *did* comic books get started? And what *were* the seven most important rules for making them? Maybe Nolan already knew those things and could tell her later.

Brian and Buzz-Bee took their places in front of two easels, each bearing an oversized pad of paper. Without a word, they started making bold black marks on each blank page. And then Vera didn't care about anything else.

Two dots became eyes. Two squiggly lines became eyebrows. Noses, chins, a few tufts of fur appeared, until suddenly a mischievous squirrel popped out from Brian's easel and a shy bunny peeked out from Buzz-Bee's.

How did they *do* that?

How could so few lines, drawn so fast, make something so alive and so real?

The other campers burst into applause as Brian and Buzz-Bee laid down their markers and gave their bows. Vera was too amazed to do anything but stare.

"Okay," Buzz-Bee said. "Your turn."

Colleen passed out sheets of paper and dropped a handful of markers on each table.

"Later on, we'll talk about creating your own characters," Buzz-Bee said. "First we just want to get your hands moving over the page so you'll see for yourselves how the simplest lines can express every feeling known to humankind—or squirrel-kind or bunny-kind. The *simpler* the drawing, the more *everyone* can look at that character and see themselves there."

Brian ripped the squirrel from his pad of paper and let the page flutter to the floor like a piece of litter. Vera thought it should be framed and put in a museum of the world's best squirrel pictures.

He turned to the new blank page. "Start with two dots, like this, for the squirrel's eyes."

Vera tried to copy his dots, but before she could check if hers were spaced too far apart on her small sheet of paper compared to his eyes on the big sheet of easel paper, he was already on to the nose, mouth, and eyebrow squiggles. Eyebrow squiggles were hard. The slightest difference in a squiggle turned excitement into fear, or fear into irritation.

Wait! she wanted to call out.

All around her, the others were drawing ten times faster than she was. Nolan copied every stroke of Brian's marker as if he were a photocopy machine. Vera could already see Nixie's cartoon eyes were too far apart, but Nixie didn't seem to care. Boogie's eyebrows made his cartoon squirrel look as if it had been electrocuted. The other two kids at their table, who were from the other two third-grade classes—a girl named Harper and a boy named James— seemed to be keeping up just fine. Only Vera was still agonizing over how to draw the eyebrows while Brian was already sketching the two curvy lines that caused a squirrel's tail to spring into existence.

"Is everyone with me?" Brian finally asked, laying down his marker for a minute.

No! Vera wanted to cry, but she couldn't bear to be the only one admitting defeat.

Buzz-Bee and Brian started circulating from table to table to check everybody's squirrels so far. Vera had no squirrel, no anything,

just two eyes and a nose she wasn't sure were exactly like they were supposed to be.

As Buzz-Bee approached Vera's table, Vera felt herself stiffening with dread.

"Nice," Buzz-Bee said to Nolan.

"My nose looks weird," Nixie complained to Buzz-Bee.

Buzz-Bee studied it. "Let's try adding another line, like this." Sure enough, with one stroke of Buzz-Bee's marker, Nixie's nose looked much much more nose-like.

"Your little fellow had quite a scare!" was all she said to Boogie.

To James she gave a nod of approval. To Harper, whose squirrel looked the most squirrelly of all, she said, "You've done some drawing like this before, haven't you?" In reply, Harper gave a shrug.

Vera wanted to cover hers up so Buzz-Bee couldn't see it, but she knew she couldn't do that, so she just sat completely still, sick with shame.

"You froze up," Buzz-Bee said matter-of-factly. "It happens."

"He went so fast," Vera managed to say.

"Fast is good," Buzz-Bee told her. "Turn off your brain. Let your eyes and hand do their thing."

Buzz-Bee stood waiting, for what Vera didn't know.

"Remember: don't think," Buzz-Bee said. "Just draw."

"Now?" Vera asked.

"Now."

But they were all staring at her—Nixie, Nolan, Boogie, Harper, and James, who seemed to be hiding a grin at Vera's predicament.

"The rest of you, go get another snack." Buzz-Bee waved them away.

"I'm not hungry," Harper said.

"Yes, you are," said Buzz-Bee.

Nixie shot Vera a sympathetic look as she turned to follow the others to the snack table. Once they had departed, Buzz-Bee repeated her command: "Draw!"

So Vera did. Sixty seconds later she had a squirrel!

"There!" Buzz-Bee patted her on the shoulder. "It doesn't have to be *perfect*. It just has to *be*."

Tell that to my mother, Vera wanted to say. *My mother has to think it's perfect or she won't let me stay.*

But the last thing in the world she wanted was for the comic-book teachers and her mother to ever meet.

☆ ☆ ☆

The comic-book part of comic-book camp ended at five. After that, kids who needed to stay longer could do homework or pretty much anything that wouldn't bother anyone else, until the program ended at six. At cooking camp, Vera's mother had been one of the come-at-six parents.

Vera was relieved that by the time her mother arrived to collect her that afternoon, Brian, Buzz-Bee, and their tattoos had already departed. She grinned at her squirrel, chicken, and elephant drawings. They were good, they really were! But even if they were as amazing as Brian's and Buzz-Bee's, they would probably still look silly to her mother. So she tucked them safely out of sight inside one of her library books for her report on the life cycle of baboons.

"How was it?" her mother asked once they were buckled into the car.

"Great! There are two teachers, Brian and Bee"—Vera was glad she hadn't let "Buzz-Bee" slip out—"and they can draw *anything*."

"What did *you* do?" her mother asked.

"We did a bunch of drawing, too. Lots of drawing, actually. Of different kinds of animals."

"So it's really more of an art class," Vera's mother said, apparently trying to reassure herself that this new camp wasn't a waste of time and money, after all.

"Yes!" Vera agreed happily.

"So that's the only thing you did for the whole time? For two entire hours?" her mother persisted. "Just sat there drawing?"

"Well, we also saw a video."

Too late Vera remembered her mother didn't believe in after-school programs that parked kids in front of a TV. "Screen time" at Vera's house was limited to half an hour a day.

"It was an educational video," Vera added. "On the history of comics as an art form."

Her mother gave a snort. But Vera had liked

the video. It had covered the blah-blah-blah on the history of comic books that Brian had skipped in an entertaining way, with animated characters doing the narration.

So far she had liked every single thing about comic-book camp. Well, she wasn't completely sure she liked Harper and James. Harper was mega-talented at drawing and clearly knew it. But maybe Vera was just jealous. And James had a smirky kind of face. But maybe that was just the way his face looked. Unless she made a special effort to smile, Vera knew her own face tended to look serious, even sad.

"Did you finish up your homework?" her mother asked then.

Vera nodded. She always used her free time after school to get her homework done.

"Well, do your piano practice, and then you can help me make dinner," her mother said. She added, "I wouldn't mind curling up in bed early tonight so we can read some extra chapters of *Roll of Thunder, Hear My Cry*."

Even though Vera could read perfectly well on her own, her mother still read to her each evening before bedtime, and it was the best part of the day.

Though maybe today it would be the second-best part of the day.

The best part was when she had drawn her squirrel and could almost feel his fluffy tail waving at her.

★ three ★

In camp on Tuesday, they spent most of the time reading and talking about a huge stack of comics and graphic novels Brian and Buzz-Bee had brought in from all over the world. Brian explained that although the terms are used by different people in different ways, "comic books" are generally installments in an ongoing story that may continue for years or even decades. "Graphic novels" are longer and more complex, telling a single story from beginning to end, the way regular novels do, except in comics format.

When her mother asked her, on the way home, what they had done at camp, Vera chose her words carefully.

"We looked at *multicultural* comics and

graphic novels." Her mother loved things that were multicultural.

But Vera could tell from the way her mother raised her eyebrows that she liked multicultural books, music, and films better than multicultural comics.

On Wednesday, Buzz-Bee said the special thing about comics was that they were made up of pictures in a *sequence*: that is, the pictures were placed one after the other, in a particular order. Comics tended to be organized in *panels* or *frames* on each page with tiny bits of white space between them. Characters talked in *speech bubbles*. *Sound effects* were things like WHAMMO! written in big bold letters so you could practically hear and feel the impact the action made in the story just by seeing how the word looked on the page.

Brian passed out a bunch of blank pages with four panels on them. The campers were supposed to decide what dialogue to put inside speech bubbles for each panel and then draw pictures and sound effects to go along with them to tell a story. It was hard but fun, like a puzzle that needs to be solved.

Nolan was the best at making everything fit neatly into each panel. Boogie kept knocking his colored pencils onto the floor and then having to hunt for them under his chair while James snickered. Nixie's speech bubbles with BOW-WOW and ARF! ARF! in huge letters took up so much space in her panels she had no room left for pictures. Harper acted bored, as if she had already done stuff like this a thousand times before.

Vera was thrilled when she finished her page, with quick sketches of dogs (Nixie had begged her to draw dogs) fitting perfectly into each panel to make a story about a new puppy arriving at Bow-Wow Academy. She did love comics so much!

On Thursday, a guest comic-book artist came to camp. He was young and funny, with a crewcut and a polka-dot bowtie. His drawings were completely different from Brian's and Buzz-Bee's: superheroes engaged in mortal combat. Watching him draw was like being in the middle of a battle. Vera didn't mention that part to her mother. Her mother thought violent comics were the worst comics of all.

On Friday, Brian started off with two announcements.

Next week the campers would begin on their big project for the camp: creating their own original comic book.

Nixie gave Vera a big smile. She leaned over and whispered, "We've started ours already!"

It was clear Nixie was still assuming the two of them would be partners. Vera didn't have an idea of her own yet that she liked better than Nixie's dog school, but what if she found one between now and then?

Brian's second announcement was that the grand camp finale would be a field trip to the opening day of a comic-book convention. He called it a comic-con.

"Hundreds of comic-book artists. Thousands of comic-book fans, many in unbelievable costumes. All together in one enormous place for a three-day spectacle," Brian said. "There's nothing else in the world like it."

The library erupted into chaos. Buzz-Bee

put her hand in the air to signal everyone to quiet down so Brian could finish talking.

"And," Brian said, "there's going to be a chance for kids your age from schools all over the country to display their work, so we'll be sending in one finished page from each of *your* comic books. A team of professional comic-book creators will award ribbons to ones they think are especially promising."

Nixie nudged Vera. "And they'll think Mistress Barker's Bow-Wow Academy on Wag-a-Tail Lane is the best comic they've ever seen, and they'll help us get it published, and we'll make a million dollars, and split it fifty-fifty, and then my parents won't be able to say we can't afford a dog!"

Vera had no choice but to return Nixie's happy grin this time. But what if she made a comic on her own, not with Nixie, and her comic somehow won a prize at the comic-con? Maybe that would make her mother glad she had let Vera do the comics camp. But it already seemed too late to tell Nixie she wanted to work alone.

Buzz-Bee had to raise her hand again to get everyone to settle down. Vera was glad when the library was quiet. She wanted to hear every detail about comic-con.

"Can we miss school to go? So we can be there the whole day?" someone at another table asked.

"No,"Buzz-Bee said."This is an *after*-school program, so the trip will have to be *after* school. We'll take a bus there as soon as school is dismissed at three and be back in the school parking lot by eight. Parents are welcome to join us, either coming along on the bus or meeting up with us later at the convention center. We're sending home permission slips for the trip today."

The mention of permission slips and parents made Vera's stomach clench in a hard knot. A comic-con definitely didn't sound like something her mother would consider an enriching activity. But if it was part of the camp, surely her mother would sign the form to let her go. Her mother always supported her participation in school activities.

But this was an *after*-school activity.

And it wasn't gymnastics, or piano, or some special math or science thing for gifted students.

It was a *comics* activity.

The knot in her stomach tightened even more.

☆ ☆ ☆

"Guess what?" Vera asked at dinner.

She had decided to wait until her mother changed from her financial-planner suit into comfy sweatpants and T-shirt, and the leftover spinach lasagna had been heated up in the microwave. She had set the table without having to be reminded. She had even folded the cloth napkins into pretty triangles and moved the vase of asters from the counter to be a centerpiece.

"What am I supposed to guess?" her mother replied.

Vera took a deep breath. Then she plunged in. "There's going to be a field trip at the end of comics camp! The coolest trip ever! To a comic-book convention! The teachers gave us the permission slip for it today!" She took it from her lap and laid it next to her mother's plate. "Here it is!"

And you're going to sign it, right? But she didn't ask that. If she didn't pose it as a question, maybe her mother couldn't give her the answer she was afraid of hearing.

Her mother swallowed another slow bite of lasagna. It was never a good sign when her mother gave a long pause before saying something.

"Honey," she said, "I don't think a comic-con"—Vera was surprised her mother knew what they were called—"is an appropriate trip for someone your age. I saw a story about them once on a news program, and there will be huge crowds of very weird people."

Vera tried to think of something she could say to convince her mother. "There's going to be prizes for the best comics by kids." Her mother had been so proud when Vera placed first for kids eight and under in a piano competition last summer. But maybe her mother wouldn't think a comics prize was the same thing as a piano prize, or a gymnastics trophy, or a school award for math or science. Besides, if any-one from their camp was going to get a rib-bon, it would probably be Harper, who already seemed to know everything there was to know about comics.

"I hate to disappoint you, honey, you know I do," her mother said. "But I have to do what I think is best."

Vera knew better than to whine or beg. If there was anything her mother hated, it was whining and begging.

So unless Vera found some other way to change her mother's mind, which had never happened before in Vera's entire life, the an-swer was no.

★ four ★

Over the weekend Vera practiced the piano an extra ten minutes each day. She made all the fact cards for her life-cycle-of-the-baboon report for Mrs. Townsend. She didn't ask if she could call Nixie for a playdate. Vera hoped her mother would notice her extra piano practice, the tidy stack of baboon fact cards, and how cheerfully she hopped into the car for gymnastics. And then her mother would say, *What was I thinking? Of course you may go to comic-con!*

But her mother didn't.

☆ ☆ ☆

"All right, artists!" Brian said, when the second week of camp began on Monday. "We're going to do some role-playing today."

"What's role-playing?" someone else asked so Vera didn't have to.

"Acting," Brian explained. "Using our faces, our bodies, our whole selves, to *show* emotion."

Vera felt her face, body, and whole self showing the emotion of hating anything to do with acting. In kindergarten, she had been a turkey in the Thanksgiving pageant. All the kindergartners had been turkeys, wearing turkey costumes made out of brown-paper grocery bags colored with markers to look like feathers. Even at age five, she had known she looked nothing like a turkey. One of the other parents had called over to her, "Cheer up, Vera! Nobody's going to be eating *you* on Thanksgiving!"

Brian kept on talking, telling them how important it was for comic-book artists to pay attention to the different ways characters showed emotion *physically*. Emotion was shown in your eyes, your shoulders, your hands, even in the way you positioned your feet.

"Take shyness," Brian said. All at once, before their eyes, he became a shy little boy with tilted head, hunched shoulders, hands hidden in his pockets, one sneaker tucked in against the other.

"Okay, we're going to start with fear," Brian continued, turning back into a grown-up comic-book teacher. "Fear is a great emotion to launch a story with, because you can show your character facing that fear and finally overcoming it by the story's end. What are some of the things you guys are afraid of? Everyone, take a piece of paper from the pile on your table and write down your three top fears."

Vera wrote:

ACTING

MATH TESTS

Vera hated when she had to answer a bunch of math questions quickly, without time to double-check her answers, and then brought home a paper with red marks scrawled all over it.

She thought for a minute before writing her third fear:

MAKING MY MOTHER MAD AT ME

Though her mother never got angry, exactly, just disappointed, which was even worse. So

Vera crossed that one out and wrote:

MAKING MY MOTHER SAD

"All right," Brian said. "I want everyone to tell me one fear from your list. Just one."

He went around the room calling on kids at top speed. The answers rang out.

"Roller coasters!"

"Snakes!"

"Spiders!"

"Aliens!"

When he turned to Vera's table, she said, "Math tests," and people laughed, in a friendly, not a mean way. It always surprised her when someone thought she was funny, especially when she hadn't meant to be.

Nixie said, "Movies where bad things happen to dogs."

Nolan said, "Falling into a hole when I'm walking along thinking about something else."

Harper said, "Spiders," which wasn't very original in Vera's opinion as three other kids had already said that.

James said, "Stepping in dog-doo," and

people laughed at that one, too. Vera had a feeling it wasn't really one of James's fears, he had just said it to get the laughs.

Boogie said, "Clowns," which seemed strange, as he would make such a great clown himself.

"Okay!" Brian said, once the last kid had spoken. "Let's go with spiders, since so many of you picked that one." Harper looked pleased, as if Brian had given her some kind of praise. "Though . . . maybe it would be more interesting to choose an unusual fear. So let's do fear of grasshoppers instead." The girl who had offered that fear beamed.

"Now for the fun part." Brian grinned at the kids. "I'm going to need a few helpers up here to act out a scene for us."

Vera shrank into her seat. *Don't pick me. Don't pick me. Don't pick me.*

Fortunately hands shot up all around the library. Brian chose four kids, including Boogie and James.

"Come on up, actors!" Brian directed. The four kids left their seats to form a group next to Brian's big drawing pad.

"So you're terrified of grasshoppers," Brian began. In a low voice he said, "It's the way they *hop*. The thought of those little feet hopping over you, and of course if this was going to be a real comic, we'd do some research into how many legs grasshoppers have. Let's say six. Six little grasshopper feet hopping all over you, and those papery grasshopper wings brushing against your bare skin."

Vera shuddered. Now she'd have to list GRASSHOPPERS as fear number four.

"So you're outside on a summer day, and the sun is shining, and the sky is blue, and then there it is: a grasshopper! Lying in wait to hop all over you! What do you do?"

One kid still stood the same way he had been standing before, with no expression on his face. Vera sympathized, but why had he volunteered to be an actor if he didn't want to act? The only girl in the group waved her hands in the air and gave a fake-sounding, too-loud-for-a-library scream. James made his mouth into a big O and clapped his hands to his cheeks, then cracked up as if he thought he was being extra-funny.

Boogie was the best. He froze in place, shoulders raised, hands dangling helplessly, mouth slightly open, eyes twitching from side to side. Vera felt even more afraid of grasshoppers just looking at him.

"Good job," Brian told the actors. "You," he said to Boogie then. "Hold that pose! The rest of you actors can go ahead and sit back down. Now, everybody, start drawing!"

Vera drew fast this time, the way Buzz-Bee had shown her, trying to capture the shape of Boogie's hunched shoulders and limp hands.

James didn't bother drawing anything. Under his breath, he muttered, "Well, it's easier to look like a fraidy-cat if you really are one."

Vera was glad to see Nixie glaring at James. Boogie *wasn't* a fraidy-cat. He was just a good actor, a hundred times better than James.

"Grasshoppers can jump twenty times the length of their bodies," Nolan said, filling the awkward moment.

James gave a huff, as if to say, *Who cares?*

Vera thought Harper's drawing of Boogie was terrific, clearly the best at their table.

She wished she could draw that well. But she was already drawing better than she had last week. Could she draw well enough by the end of camp to win a prize at comic-con?

Maybe her comic could still be shown at comic-con even if she wasn't there.

But it wouldn't be *hers*. It would be hers and Nixie's, and mostly Nixie's because the doggy school had been Nixie's idea in the first place.

It wouldn't count as *Vera's* prize. Not that she'd even be there to see it.

☆ ☆ ☆

"A character in a comic can be anybody," Buzz-Bee said on Tuesday. "Anybody or anything can be a character in a story. It might be a human. Or it might be a dog."

Nixie gave Vera's arm a poke.

"Or someone who's part human, part dog. Or a unicorn. What else? You don't have to raise your hands. Just call out ideas."

"A skateboard!"

"A pillow!"

"Dust bunnies!"

"Boogers!"

"That's right," Buzz-Bee said. "You get the idea. And every character has to have a *problem.* You don't have a story if there's no problem your main character is facing. The bigger the problem, the more exciting the story. To spark your imaginations, I'm going to pass around index cards. You'll each get two. One of the cards will have the name of an object like *skateboard, pillow, booger.*" She smiled at the kid who had said boogers.

"The other card will have an adjective—a describing word—like *scared, angry, embarrassed, brave.* Your job is to draw something that combines the words from the two cards. Draw a scared pillow or a brave booger. And think about—and start drawing if you can— what *makes* your pillow scared. *Why* does your booger need to be brave? That will point you toward your character's problem. Got it?"

Vera's mother didn't even like the word *booger.* She would hardly appreciate entire conversations about the problems of boogers.

As Brian began handing out the cards,

Buzz-Bee added, "Don't worry about making your drawing perfect." She turned toward Vera's table as she said it. "Just think of this as the seed of a *story*."

Vera felt nervous as she took the two cards Brian gave her: *frightened* and *spoon*.

How would you draw a frightened spoon?

And what would a spoon be frightened of? Probably not roller coasters, snakes, spiders, or grasshoppers.

What if she was the only one at her table who couldn't think of anything to draw?

"I got *silly* and *Popsicle*," Nixie said. "Did any of you get an animal on your card, like a dog?"

Nixie was definitely obsessed with dogs.

"I got *stubborn* and *shoe*," said Nolan. "Velcro is sort of stubborn, the way it sticks and sticks, sometimes to things you don't want it to stick to. Did you know the person who invented Velcro got the idea from burrs that stuck to his dog's fur when they went for a walk in the woods?"

Nolan definitely had facts about absolutely everything.

"I got *sympathetic* and *toaster*," Boogie said mournfully. "I could imagine a *sad* toaster, like maybe he's sad because nobody in his family likes eating toast, so he gets dusty and rusty. But a *sympathetic* toaster?"

Harper got *angry* and *watermelon*. She had already started on her drawing as if nothing was easier than to draw a slice of watermelon in a rage.

James got *conceited* and *lightbulb*. Vera saw him look right at Nolan when he read his cards aloud. She had to admit Nolan was sort of like a lightbulb, the way his eyes would shine whenever a fascinating fact popped into his head. But he wasn't a *conceited* lightbulb, just a supersmart one.

"Some talking can be helpful," Buzz-Bee said, "to start brainstorming ideas. But now it's time to switch from busy mouths to busy hands."

Vera stared down at her paper. Why would a spoon be frightened? It was a little spoon, she decided, a baby-food spoon, scared of a bigger spoon—one of those huge wooden spoons her mother used to stir things on the stove.

She picked up her pencil and started to draw, and then she couldn't stop.

Big Spoon was stirring lasagna sauce on the stove. Little Spoon was trying to help, but she kept getting in the way, because the sauce was deeper than the tip of her handle. Finally, Little Spoon started drowning. "Help! Help!" Little Spoon cried, swallowing sauce every time she opened her mouth. Then Big Spoon rescued Little Spoon, washed her off in the sink, and put her in the dish rack to dry.

Was that enough of a story to make a good comic? Buzz-Bee had said the main character in any story had to have a *problem.* The bigger the problem, the more exciting the story.

Was drowning in a pot of lasagna sauce a big enough problem for an exciting story?

Well, it was if you were Little Spoon.

And Little Spoon had looked so ashamed, all alone in the dish rack, and Big Spoon had looked so cross as she kept on stirring.

Vera couldn't help wanting to know what would happen to Little Spoon and Big Spoon next.

★ five ★

"**A**ll right, campers," Buzz-Bee said on Wednesday. "It's time for you to start working on the actual comic book you're going to be making for your big camp project."

"Can we work with partners?" Boogie asked right away.

Say no! Vera beamed the answer to Buzz-Bee.

"Sure!" Buzz-Bee said. Vera stifled a sigh. "But just one partner, not your entire table. Or you can work alone, of course."

"*I'm* working alone," Harper announced. Her tone suggested no one else was up to her level.

"Me too," James said. Vera doubted anyone would want to work with someone who smirked all the time.

"Can we be partners?" Boogie asked Nolan.

Nolan gave a big thumbs-up in reply.

How could Boogie and Nolan possibly work together? Boogie was messy. Nolan was neat. Nolan would want their book to be filled with fascinating facts. Boogie would want their book to make everybody laugh out loud.

"Vera and I are working together on a dog comic," Nixie said happily.

This was Vera's last chance to say something. *Actually, Nixie, if it's okay with you, I'd rather work alone. The dog-school idea is so great, but it was your idea, and I want to work on an idea all my own.* Suddenly she knew what the idea was, too: she wanted to make her big project about Little Spoon and Big Spoon.

But Nixie was Vera's only real friend so far at Longwood. Nixie always said things to make Vera feel special, like when she had told Vera she was good at bowling, which was completely not true. Vera couldn't disappoint Nixie or make her feel rejected.

"Right, Vera?" Nixie persisted.

Vera forced a smile. Had Nolan had to force his smile, too?

"Right!" she made herself say.

☆ ☆ ☆

Even if Vera had to be Nixie's partner on the Mistress Barker's Bow-Wow Academy comic, that didn't mean she couldn't keep on drawing Little Spoon and Big Spoon.

So for the rest of the week, in the extra time at the end of camp, after her homework was done and Nixie had already been picked up by her mom or dad, Vera drew spoons. She drew them at home, too, when her mother was busy working so Vera could be sure of being undisturbed. Nobody else needed to know what Little Spoon was doing.

Maybe she should call her comic *The Secret Life of Little Spoon.*

Ooh! That was a great title, in Vera's opinion.

Big Spoon never wanted Little Spoon to go out of the silverware drawer by herself, but Little Spoon did sometimes. Little Spoon made friends with Plastic Spoon, who she met on the counter; Big Spoon didn't approve of plastic spoons. Little Spoon also made friends with Chopsticks, left over from a Chinese takeout

dinner. Little Spoon, Plastic Spoon, and Chopsticks had all kinds of adventures. The best one was saving Teaspoon from falling into the garbage disposal. Plastic Spoon and Chopsticks helped with the rescues, but the bravest rescuer was Little Spoon.

The special camp activity on Thursday was going outside with sketch pads to get ideas to add to their stories. Nixie spent most of her time drawing the collie and beagle who lived in the backyard next door, while Vera drew the slide, the swings, the monkey bars, and the teeter-totter. Maybe she should start sending Little Spoon outdoors for her feats of daring. There was a whole big world beyond the kitchen for Little Spoon to see.

On Friday, Brian and Buzz-Bee told the campers they could spend the entire camp time working on their comics.

"What kind of criminal should our dogs bring to justice?" Nixie asked Vera as they sat side by side looking through the pictures they had drawn already. So far the pile had lots of scenes of the dogs—Tootles the terrier, Cora the corgi, Sparky the spaniel, Sir Great the Great

Dane, and Itty-Bitty the Chihuahua—playing at the academy, but they didn't have a real story yet, with a problem to be solved. It was definitely time for the dogs to start fighting crime on Wag-a-Tail Lane.

"A cat?" Vera suggested. She knew Nixie didn't like cats, so Nixie might think a cat would make the perfect criminal.

Nixie shook her head. "It wouldn't take five dogs to defeat one little cat."

"This wouldn't have to be a *little* cat," Vera said.

"Yes!" Nixie's face lit up. "It could be a cat that somehow got very, very big. How could a cat turn into a giant cat?" she asked Nolan.

"Humans become giants if their pituitary gland produces too much growth hormone," Nolan said. "But giant humans aren't *that* much bigger than normal-size ones."

"The giant cat has to be humongous," Nixie said. "So that pit-something gland would have to make tons and tons of growth hormone. What could make it do that?"

Nolan gave a friendly shrug. Maybe he didn't know *everything*.

"The cat gets struck by lightning," Boogie called over from the snack table. Once the campers had started working on their big projects, Colleen had made a rule of no snacks at the work tables; kids could still grab snacks whenever they wanted if they stayed a safe distance away from everyone's work to eat them.

"But instead of getting killed," Boogie went on, "it gets *zapped*. Zapped right in that gland. And then"—he drew closer to their table and made his voice low and mysterious—"it starts to grow. And grow. And grow. And it turns out getting zapped not only makes cats get big. It makes them turn evil, too."

"Yay!" Nixie cheered. "You guys are the best!"

Nolan and Boogie's comic wasn't the best, though. Boogie and Nolan each did their own part, and neither part had much to do with the other one. Boogie's part was about a toaster—not a sympathetic toaster, but a klutzy one. Each time a piece of bread was put into the toaster, the toaster would make a big smiley face and say, "No more klutziness for me! *This* time the toast is going to land on the *plate!*"

The next frame of the comic would show the toast shouting, *"Oops!"* as he flew off to the places Nolan had drawn: the moon, or Mount Everest, or the Great Wall of China. Then Nolan added a bunch of facts, like how the moon was 238,855 miles from Earth. Or how, in 1953, Tenzing Norgay and Sir Edmund Hillary were the first climbers known to reach the summit of Mount Everest.

The title of the comic was *Oops!*

Actually, Vera had to admit Boogie and Nolan's comic was pretty funny. And educational, too.

Vera didn't know what Harper's comic was about. Harper circled her arm around her pieces of paper as she drew, as if to keep the others from stealing her brilliant ideas. James had started doing that, too. He gave little snorts of laughter as he drew, though, so his comic was probably hilarious, or at least he thought it was. When Brian or Buzz-Bee came by to offer assistance, Harper let them look at her work, but nobody else. James didn't even let the teachers look. He said he wanted his to be a surprise.

"How do you spell *pituitary gland*?" he asked Nolan now.

Nolan looked startled. Vera was puzzled, too. Why on earth would James want to know *that*?

"P-i-t-u-i-t-a-r-y-space-g-l-a-n-d," Nolan spelled.

James wrote it down, chuckling to himself as if no word in the history of the world had ever been spelled in such a comical way.

"Do you want to be the one to draw Evil Giant Cat or should I?" Nixie asked Vera.

Another problem of working together with Nixie was that they didn't draw in the same style. In a dog comic, the dogs shouldn't look different on different pages, but with two people drawing, a dog drawn by Nixie didn't look the same as a dog drawn by Vera. Vera was drawing Sir Great and Itty-Bitty, while Nixie drew the other three. It made everything more complicated.

If only Vera was brave enough to tell Nixie she wanted to do her own comic by herself!

But she couldn't hurt Nixie's feelings; she just couldn't.

"I'll draw Evil Giant Cat," Vera said. That seemed fair. "Then you'll have three characters to draw, and I'll have three."

But in her heart the only character Vera wanted to be drawing was Little Spoon.

★ six ★

Vera hadn't mentioned comic-con to her mother since the first time she had brought it up a week ago and her mother had said no. She had already stopped practicing the piano for an extra ten minutes a day. As far as she could tell, her mother hadn't even noticed.

Her mother did notice the A+ Vera got on her life-cycle-of-the-baboon report, which she brought home after camp on Friday afternoon.

"Oh, this is splendid, honey!" her mother had said. She had propped the report, with its big bold A+ on the cover, up on the fireplace mantel.

As she joined her mother at the kitchen table for dinner, Vera wondered if this was a good time to ask about comic-con again. Her mother was definitely in a good mood from the A+.

But Vera didn't.

She just wanted to see her mother smile as she gazed at the report every time she walked into the living room.

☆ ☆ ☆

Nixie came over on Sunday afternoon so they could work on their comic together. Vera wished she was going to Nixie's house, but Vera's mother had said it was easier to have Nixie come there. Vera had a feeling it was because if Vera's family hosted first, Nixie's family would be the one that had to worry about "reciprocating." But Nixie's family didn't seem to worry about things as much as Vera's mother did.

If Vera's father hadn't died all those years ago, would her mother have worried less?

If her father had been there now, would he have told her mom, *Oh, just let her go to comic-con, hon*?

Would he have thought comics were terrific, or even if he didn't, would he have loved them just because Vera did?

Some things Vera would never know.

As soon as Nixie arrived, she dashed up to Vera's room as if she had been to Vera's house a hundred times. She flung herself onto Vera's bed, not even caring if she rumpled the bedspread dotted with tiny blue violets.

"Let's look at your animal encyclopedia!" Nixie said.

Vera didn't say, *I thought we were supposed to be working on our comic.* It was getting harder and harder to pretend she liked drawing the doggy students at Mistress Barker's Academy.

"There's this dog I saw on a TV show last night," Nixie went on. "I forget the name of the breed, so I want to see if I can find it in your book."

Vera lifted the book from her bedside table and set it on the bed beside Nixie.

"Where's the section on dogs?" Nixie asked. She started to leaf through the pages. "What's this?" she asked, holding up a sheaf of papers.

Vera remembered she had hurriedly tucked some of the Little Spoon drawings into the book last night just as her mother had come in for their bedtime reading. Oh, well, the drawings didn't have to be a secret from Nixie, even though the comic was called *The Secret Life* of *Little Spoon*. Still, Vera's heart beat faster as Nixie examined the first few drawings. Little Spoon was so . . . little . . . and . . . scared so much of the time, even when she made herself be brave. Vera's heart would break if Nixie tossed Little Spoon aside as if the drawings were boring compared to a bunch of dog photos in an animal book.

But when Nixie looked up, her eyes glowed.

"Vera," she said solemnly. "These are *wonderful*."

Vera found her voice. "They are?"

"They are super-duper, extra-terrific, best-comics-in-the-world wonderful." Nixie gave emphasis to every word.

"But . . . you said my *bowling* was great, too. And it was *terrible*."

Nixie brushed Vera's comment aside with a wave of her hand. "Okay, I said that about the bowling to make you feel better. I'm telling the truth now. Vera, *this* is the comic you should be making for camp. Not Mistress Barker's Bow-Wow Academy. *This* one about the spoons."

Vera and Nixie hugged each other hard.

"Do you really mean it?" Vera asked.

"Totally! But is it okay if I still do the Bow-Wow comic? Even though you named the school, and thought of Wag-a-Tail Lane, and helped think up the characters, and everything?"

Vera could feel her own eyes shining. "Of course!"

"Now I'll get to draw Evil Giant Cat! She was the one I wanted to draw most, but I didn't want to take her away from you!"

Vera heard her mother's footsteps coming down the hall. Quickly, she positioned the book on top of the pile of Little Spoon pictures.

"If you girls want a snack, let me know," Vera's mother offered as she came into the room. "We don't bring snacks into the bedroom, but you could spread out your project on the dining room table if you'd like to work there."

Vera shot a panicked glance at Nixie.

"We're fine," Nixie answered for both of them. "Thanks, though!"

Vera waited to see if her mother would ask to see their comics. To her great relief, she didn't.

"All right, girls," was all she said. "Have fun!" The door closed behind her with a gentle *click*.

"Now," Nixie said, the animal book apparently forgotten, "let's draw!"

★ seven ★

A hero's journey, Vera learned on Monday, begins with the "call to adventure." Those were such tingly words they gave her a thrill.

Buzz-Bee was telling them about a man named Joseph Campbell who wrote a book called *The Hero with a Thousand Faces*. The title meant there were thousands of stories about all different kinds of heroes, but every hero story had the same basic structure, or shape. That's what made them *hero* stories.

The hero's story had so many parts probably even Nolan couldn't remember them all. Buzz-Bee told the students how the hero's story starts with regular, ordinary, everyday life. Then the "call to adventure" comes, although sometimes the hero doesn't want to answer it. Of course the hero does eventually respond, or else he or she wouldn't turn out to be a hero. Then the hero finds "mentors" (wise advisers) and other helpers, and faces a bunch of tests and challenges, leading up to one huge test, the "supreme ordeal." The hero succeeds and then goes back home to regular, ordinary, everyday life again. But the hero is changed in some way because of everything that has happened in the story.

Vera gave a sigh of satisfaction when Buzz-Bee finished talking. The words Buzz-Bee had used were so grand and glorious. They made Vera want to be a hero herself, not now, of course, because third-graders didn't get calls to go on adventures, and her mother wouldn't let her answer a call to adventure, anyway. But someday.

Then she thought about her own comic and felt a stab of worry.

Little Spoon had no call to adventure. She just fell out of the silverware drawer when she was being put away from the dishwasher.

Little Spoon had no real mentors or helpers, just Plastic Spoon and Chopsticks, and they were often as lost and frightened as Little Spoon herself.

Little Spoon did have adventures, but just the same kind of little adventures one after the other. Her story had no supreme ordeal, just little ordeals, which might make sense for a little spoon, but not for a true hero on a true hero's journey.

If Joseph Campbell was right, Vera's comic was wrong.

She had never raised her hand in comics camp, but this time, when Buzz-Bee asked if anybody had any questions, hers was the first hand to go up.

"What if your comic-book character doesn't do *any* of those things?" She could hear the wobble in her voice.

"Well," Buzz-Bee said, "not all comics are hero stories. Think back to the examples we shared the first week. Plenty of comics just show funny little things that happen in real life, and that's completely fine. But I have a feeling, when all of you look again at the comics you're making, you'll likely find your hero *does* do many of these things, in his or her own way."

Was that true of Little Spoon?

Maybe falling out of a drawer *was* a call to adventure, especially if you had never been out of a drawer on your own before.

Maybe a plastic spoon *could* be a mentor and a pair of chopsticks *could* be a helper.

But Little Spoon definitely kept having the same kind of small adventures over and over again. Vera knew that for sure.

"Besides," Buzz-Bee continued, "the whole reason we're talking about the hero's journey is to help us decide how best to tell our stories. If your story lacks one of these elements, guess what? You can change your story. You can revise your story—any story—to add whatever you think is missing. It's as simple as that."

Buzz-Bee smiled at Vera, and Vera gave her an even bigger smile in return.

Now all she had to do was give Little Spoon a supreme ordeal, an adventure bigger than all the other ones, which all the little adventures would have been preparing her for.

Little Spoon needed to perform some great big, extra-heroic rescue.

Little Spoon needed to rescue the entire silverware drawer.

Little Spoon needed to rescue . . . Big Spoon.

☆ ☆ ☆

"I don't think our comic is a hero's journey, do you?" Boogie asked Nolan during camp the next day, as everyone got out their comics to work on them some more. "I mean, our toaster keeps popping up a piece of toast, and the toast lands somewhere crazy, and the toaster says 'Oops!', and there's a bunch of facts, and then there's another piece of bread in the toaster, and it starts all over again."

Nolan nodded thoughtfully. "Ours is more of a nonfiction comic. The toast part is there just to make it fun for kids to read."

Boogie looked relieved.

"*Mine* is a hero's journey," Harper said, tossing back her long, dark brown hair.

Vera wanted to ask, *What happens in yours?* But maybe Harper would say, *None of your business*, and hide her papers even more so no one could see.

Then Nolan asked Harper, "What happens in yours?" That was probably why he knew so many things. He never minded asking questions other people were afraid to ask.

Harper hesitated. Then, as if figuring the rest of them were going to find out sooner or later, she said, "It's about Princess Esmerelda of the kingdom of Esmer, and her call to adventure is when the Ancient Ones come to her and tell her that because she was born in the eighth minute of the eighth day of the eighth month of the year 8,888, she is the only one who can save her people from being wiped off the face of her planet."

It sounded so much like a real comic that Vera felt even sadder for Little Spoon, whose call to adventure had been so much less dignified.

"Mine's going to have a call to adventure when Evil Giant Cat arrives," Nixie said. "Right now the dogs are having so much fun at Bow-Wow Academy I haven't made it happen yet."

"Mine has *no* call to adventure," James said, as if this made his comic vastly better than theirs. "Mine is just funny." He shot a glance at Nolan and Boogie. "Like, really funny."

Did he mean his comic was funnier than *Oops*? Without having seen a single drawing by James, Vera already liked *Oops* better than his.

She didn't share anything about hers, not that it was a secret—she had worked on it in front of everybody yesterday—but because she couldn't bear to see Harper's superior smile or James's smirk.

"I'm hungry," Boogie declared. "You can only draw so many pieces of toast without wanting to eat something." He hopped up and got himself a paper cup of lemonade and another of Goldfish crackers.

"Hey, Boogie!" James called over to him. "Bet you can't toss a Goldfish in the air and catch it in your mouth!"

Boogie grinned at the challenge. Moving closer, he set his lemonade on top of the low bookcase next to their table, tossed a Goldfish cracker into the air—and missed.

"You lose!" James called over to him.

"That was just my warm-up," Boogie replied. "It wasn't the *real* Goldfish-cracker toss."

The second toss must not have been the real one, either, because Boogie missed that one, too.

Deep in conversation with Brian and Buzz-Bee about some camp stuff, Colleen wasn't noticing Boogie's attempts to answer James's dare. Shouldn't somebody tell Boogie to stand farther away? But Vera liked Boogie too much to say anything that might come out sounding like a criticism.

"*This* is going to be the real toss!" Boogie boasted. "Prepare to be amazed!"

The third Goldfish soared higher into the air than the first two. Trying to catch it, Boogie made a grand leap toward the bookcase.

The bookcase where his cup of lemonade was sitting.

The bookcase where his cup of lemonade *used* to be sitting.

The cup—and its contents—went flying toward their worktable.

Harper shrieked, snatching Princess Esmerelda to safety in the nick of time. Vera and Nixie, at the other end of the table, were far enough away that Nixie's dogs and Vera's spoons were spared. James didn't seem to care if his "really funny" comic got splattered.

But Boogie and Nolan's comic was drenched: lemonade had soaked through the pages of Nolan's carefully lettered facts and Boogie's drawings of the flying toast with its funny expression of wide-eyed horror at yet another mishap.

Colleen, Brian, and Buzz-Bee were there now with a roll of paper towels to soak up the lemonade.

"*This* is why we have a rule about no snacks by the worktable," Colleen scolded, stating the obvious.

All Boogie could say, in a small un-Boogie-like voice, was, "Oops."

But his eyes scrunched up and his lips twisted as if he was about to cry.

★ eight ★

At camp on Wednesday, Thursday, and Friday, Nolan and Boogie worked as hard as they could in the time left to redraw the pictures ruined by the lemonade catastrophe.

"I'm such a klutz," Boogie kept moaning.

"Look, the pictures are turning out even better this time," Nolan reassured him on Friday. "It's like those were the warm-up pictures, and these are the *real* pictures."

That sounded so much like Boogie talking about the warm-up Goldfish-cracker toss versus the *real* Goldfish-cracker toss that Boogie gave another moan.

"I'm a klutzy klutz," he said dolefully. "I'm the klutzy king of klutzy klutzes."

Vera was working even harder than Nolan and Boogie, trying to finish the drawings of

Little Spoon's biggest adventure. She almost wished Brian and Buzz-Bee hadn't shown a video on Thursday about famous comic-book heroes like Batman, Superman, Spider-Man, and Wonder Woman, and that another guest speaker hadn't come for the first part of today's camp to talk about animation. It was hard to take a whole hour each day away from drawing. But even drawing time wasn't as wonderful as it should have been because the others kept talking about comic-con, comic-con, comic-con.

☆ ☆ ☆

Ask her again, Vera told herself Saturday morning as she and her mother climbed into the car to go to gymnastics.

Why would she say anything different this time? Vera asked herself.

Maybe if you keep on asking, she'll know you really, really, REALLY want to go, Vera answered her own question.

Vera already knew what to say back to that. *When was the last time your mom ever changed her mind about anything?*

So that was the end of the silent conversation between Vera and Vera.

On the ride to the gymnastics studio and on the ride home again, she and her mother talked about everything except comic-con: how Vera had been picked for a special math class, what Scarlatti sonatina she'd be working on next in piano, and what book they should read together now that they had finished *Roll of Thunder, Hear My Cry* and were halfway through *A Wrinkle in Time*. Her mother had seen good things on a mother-daughter book-club blog about *One Crazy Summer*.

"Well, just one more week of this camp, and then on to the next one!" her mother said cheerfully, as if that was supposed to be a good thing.

It wasn't for Vera.

☆ ☆ ☆

"All right," Buzz-Bee said on Monday. "Today is the day for sharing the one page of your comic you're going to be sending off to display at comic-con. This is your chance to get *constructive* criticism from your peers. Then you can use that feedback to do any revisions you want to do before Brian and I send off your work after camp on Wednesday, to be judged on Thursday, before comic-con begins on Friday."

Every single thing Buzz-Bee said made Vera's heart twist inside her.

She didn't want "constructive criticism" on Little Spoon from any peers except for Nixie, and maybe Boogie and Nolan. Definitely not from Harper or James.

She didn't want to hear how wonderful and perfect Princess Esmerelda was. She already knew how wonderful and perfect Harper's comic was; she didn't need to hear other people say it over and over again.

And every mention of comic-con made her want to plug her fingers in her ears and leave them there forever. While the others were having a glorious time at comic-con, she'd be doing homework at the little table in the corner of her mother's downtown office.

Brian had some way of taking drawings and projecting them onto a blank wall of the library. He told the campers to bring their comic pages to the library's circular storytelling area, where they had watched the camp's videos. With her Little Spoon page clutched tightly, Vera made sure she was sitting next to Nixie.

Vera had picked a page from the beginning of the story, an improved version of her very first Little Spoon drawing: Big Spoon rescuing Little Spoon from the spaghetti sauce, but then scolding her for not being more careful. Unless people knew how the story started, they wouldn't know why it was so important for Little Spoon to be the one who rescues Big Spoon in the end.

She listened as Buzz-Bee explained the rules for critique:

Say something positive first.

Be specific. Don't just say *I liked it* or *I liked everything!* Say what in *particular* you liked.

Word any critical comments as suggestions, not statements. Don't say, *This drawing is confusing.* Instead say, *Maybe you could make what's happening here more clear.*

Vera's heart squeezed tight inside her chest.

"Okay," Brian finally said. He pointed to a boy in the front row. "You're up."

That boy's comic page first showed a flying rabbit soaring over a sleeping city. Then the rabbit landed next to a masked porcupine that was getting ready to rob a bank. (Vera knew it was a bank because a sign on the building said BANK.) The rabbit waved a weapon that looked like a flaming carrot and shouted to the porcupine, "I told you not to mess with the Bunny of Doom!"

One camper said he liked the rabbit's cool name. Another suggested that maybe the rabbit's ears could be longer so he'd look more like a rabbit and less like a guinea pig.

The next two comics were also from kids at other worktables.

Then it was Boogie and Nolan's turn. Their flying toast appeared on the wall. Vera was glad that the expression of shocked disappointment on the toast's face when it landed on the moon instead of a plate was so funny that the campers burst out laughing.

Vera wanted to say to James, *See? I bet their comic is a hundred times funnier than yours!* Of course she didn't.

Two kids later, it was Harper's turn. Her drawings of the Ancient Ones calling Esmerelda to adventure were so well drawn, with so much detail, that for the first time nobody could think of a single criticism. One kid said Harper's comic looked like it was made by a grown-up. Another said when Harper was a famous comic-book artist, he wanted her autograph.

Vera expected Harper to receive her compliments with a toss of her long hair as if she was a princess herself accepting the cheers of her humble subjects. Instead Vera heard her breathe out a long sigh of what sounded like relief. How could *Harper* be nervous about constructive criticism?

Then Vera's heart stopped beating. Brian was pointing at her.

A long moment later, there was Little Spoon projected onto the wall, covered with spaghetti sauce, looking so small and worried with her wide eyes and crooked eyebrows, as Big Spoon loomed disapprovingly.

"Awww!" came a chorus of appreciation from her fellow campers.

"She's so cute!" one of them said, without even waiting to be called on by Buzz-Bee.

No one had any critical comments about Little Spoon either, not even Harper or James.

"They loved Little Spoon!" Nixie whispered to Vera. "I told you so! Didn't I tell you? I told you she was wonderful!"

"They loved Harper's better," Vera whispered back.

"*I* didn't! I bet a grown-up did draw Harper's. I bet her parents helped her. Little Spoon is like—it's like she's a real person, a kid just like us, scared that somebody bigger is going to yell at her. Even though she's only a spoon!"

Vera hardly noticed what the next few comics were, or what anybody said about them. Sixteen pages of comics was a lot of comics to critique. Some kids were starting to squirm. How lucky Vera was that her critique was already over with!

Then Nixie, whose dogs hadn't been shown yet, gave her a hard nudge. On the wall, instead of the doggy students of Bow-Wow Academy, Vera saw a drawing of two kids. One was tubby with untamed curls standing up from his head as if he had been electrocuted. Exaggerated teardrops flew from his face as if his head was raining.

The speech bubble coming from his mouth in one panel said, "Why am I such a big fat klutz? Our comic is ruined now! WAAHH!!!"

The other kid in the picture was colored in to look darker-skinned. In another panel his speech bubble said, "It must be your PITU-ITARY GLAND! I know 10,000 boring facts about the pituitary gland! Let me tell you all of them!"

For a second no one said anything.

Then Vera sprang from her sitting position, angrier than she had ever been at anybody in her whole entire life.

"That's *mean*! It's not *funny*! It's not funny at *all*! It's nothing but mean, mean, mean, mean, MEAN!"

So much for constructive criticism.

So much for starting with something positive.

So much for making a suggestion and not a statement.

Vera didn't care.

Now Nixie was on her feet, too.

"You're just jealous because Boogie is funnier than you are, and Nolan is smarter than you are. They're funnier and smarter than you'll ever be!"

"Girls!" Buzz-Bee interrupted, sounding agitated herself. "Sit down, both of you. Let Brian and me handle this."

Vera stole a glance at Boogie and Nolan. Boogie wasn't crying, but his cheeks were bright red. Nolan's lips were pressed tightly together as if he was trying hard not to speak. Vera bet he could think of 10,000 choice facts to share with James right now.

For a moment the whole camp was silent.

Then Buzz-Bee said, "James, this 'comic' of yours . . ."

With all eyes on him, James flushed almost as red as Boogie. "You're the ones who said we should *observe* people to get *ideas*! I was trying to be funny!"

"There's a difference," Buzz-Bee said, "between *funny* and *mean*."

It was the same thing Vera had just said. But

what made them different? She didn't think her Buzz-Bee nickname was mean. Was it? If she had drawn the cartoon of Buzz-Bee that had popped into her head on the first day of camp, with Buzz-Bee's head extra-round like a bowling ball and her hair extra-short, would that have been mean?

"But Boogie *is* a big klutz! He even says that he is! He *did* ruin their comic! That really happened! Nolan *does* know facts about everything! He's the one who told me how to spell the name of that stupid gland. How can something be mean if it's *true*?"

"There's a difference," Buzz-Bee said, "between saying what's true and saying it in a way that's kind. And I think you'd have to admit your comic strays considerably far from the truth. Neither Nolan nor Boogie ever said the exact words you put in your speech bubbles. They wouldn't have. And you knew that."

Now James looked close to tears himself. "Comics are supposed to be exaggerated! That's what makes them *funny*!"

Vera almost felt sorry for him, but if he had

really thought his comic was perfectly fine, he wouldn't have covered it up every time Brian and Buzz-Bee came by their table. If he had truly thought it was a friendly joke, he would have let Nolan and Boogie see it, too, so they could have cracked up together.

"Look," Brian cut in. "Bee and I messed up on this one. We're not big on rules, as you know. Our only goal was to get you kids fired up about comics, the thing in the world both of us love best. We should have had a rule against making comics about other kids in the camp. Boogie and Nolan, we're sorry."

Would Brian make James apologize to Boogie and Nolan, too?

He didn't. Anyway, Vera always thought it was pointless when grown-ups made kids say *I'm sorry* when they didn't mean it.

"We still have five more comics to critique," Brian said. "We'll do them first thing tomorrow, when we're fresh. That's it for today, guys. I'm done."

The campers stayed quiet as they returned to their tables for free time.

Then James cleared his throat. "Nolan?

Boogie?" he said, avoiding their eyes. "If my comic was mean, I'm sorry, okay?"

"Okay," Nolan said quietly.

"Sure," Boogie agreed.

"But . . . you guys *are* funny," James added.

It was a pretty terrible apology, Vera decided, one of the worst she'd ever heard. The strange thing was: Boogie and Nolan *were* funny, Boogie always dropping things, Nolan with his facts that *were* boring sometimes. But they were even funnier because they were best friends who were completely opposite from each other.

Even in this last week of comics camp, there was so much Vera still didn't understand about comics.

★ nine ★

When the last five comics were critiqued in camp on Tuesday, everyone liked Nixie's. Vera felt bad that one person said her favorite part was that the school was called Mistress Barker's Bow-Wow Academy and that the street was called Wag-a-Tail Lane. Nixie didn't seem to mind.

During drawing time after the critiques, James just sat and sulked. But on Wednesday, he told the others he was making a brand-new comic about a turtle whose superpower was moving so slowly he went backward in time.

"You're never going to get a page finished in time for Brian and Bee to send to comic-con," Harper pointed out. "They're collecting them in an *hour*."

James shrugged. "So? This isn't *school*. It's

after school. It's just a dumb place for kids to go while their parents are at work. It's not like the stuff we do here *matters*."

Well, Vera thought, it did matter if you hurt somebody else's feelings while you were doing it.

"Does your turtle have a name?" Boogie asked. It was the first time any of them, except for Harper, had spoken to James since Monday.

James shrugged again. Apparently naming the comic-book character in your dumb after-school camp was another thing that didn't matter.

"You could call him Backwards Benny," Boogie suggested.

"Hey! That's a great name!" James gave Boogie a grin that was a smile, not a smirk.

"Did you know that turtles—" Nolan began, and then broke off.

"That turtles what?" James asked.

"Boring turtle fact," Nolan said quietly.

James flushed. "That turtles what?" he asked again. "Come on, just tell us."

"That turtles have been around for over two hundred million years." Nolan said it in a flat, expressionless voice; Vera could tell James's mockery still stung. Then his face lit up in his usual excited-lightbulb way. "Turtles have been around since the time of the dinosaurs!"

"So if Backwards Benny went back to dinosaur time," James said, "he could meet his own great-great-great-great-add-a-million-greats-turtle-grandfather."

"Yup," Nolan replied.

"Cool!" James picked up his pencil to draw some more.

"Speaking of cool," Boogie said, "are any of you going to wear costumes to comic-con on Friday? All I have is an old Superman cape from when I was, like, three or something. I asked my mother if she could make me a giant-piece-of-toast costume, and she said, 'You're kidding, right?'"

"I'm going to wear a princess costume," Harper announced. "In honor of Princess Esmeralda of Esmer. Besides, it's an amazing princess dress, and there aren't a lot of places I can wear it to now that I'm not a little kid anymore."

"I'm not a costume person," Nolan said, unsurprisingly.

"I'd rather just look at everyone else," Nixie said.

James nodded his agreement.

The others looked over at Vera, the only one who hadn't spoken. She hadn't told anyone yet that she wasn't going to comic-con, not even Nixie. It would make it too real to say it out loud. But comic-con was just two days away. She might as well blurt it out now and get it over with.

"I'm not going."

Five pairs of eyes stared at her.

"My mother said no."

Five faces looked sympathetic. Vera hadn't expected Harper or James to care either way, but James rolled his eyes in a friendly way, as if to say, *Parents!* Harper gave Vera a small, sad smile.

"What if Brian and Bee talked to her?" Nolan asked. Vera could have guessed he'd be the first one, faced with her problem, to try to think of a solution.

Vera shook her head.

"What if—what if—well, what if . . ." Boogie was obviously stuck on how to finish the sentence.

Nixie raised her chin, clearly not ready to give up yet. "What if *you* talked to her?"

"I already did."

"What if you talked to her *again*? You have to stand up for yourself when there's something you really, really, REALLY want."

Vera didn't bother answering that one. She knew Nixie wanted to help, but Nixie's own begging and pleading had never yet convinced Nixie's parents to let her get a dog.

Anyway, Vera was hopeless at standing up for herself. She hadn't been able to make herself tell Nixie she didn't want to work together on the dog comic. She'd still be drawing Sir Great the Great Dane and Itty-Bitty the Chihuahua if Nixie hadn't stumbled upon Vera's hidden drawings and told her she should make Little Spoon her big camp project.

Well, maybe she *had* stood up to James yesterday. But that didn't count. It was easier to stand up *for* someone other than herself. And it was easier to stand up *to* someone other than her mom.

When it was time for a snack break, Nixie motioned to Vera to stay behind at the worktable while the other four jumped up to get cheddar cheese slices and apple wedges.

"What if *I* talked to your mother?" Nixie persisted.

This was the most preposterous plan yet, but Vera loved Nixie for offering it.

"Oh, Nixie." Vera couldn't keep the despair out of her voice. "My mother isn't going to listen to you, or me, or the teachers, or anybody."

Nixie sighed. "You need a superhero."

Vera sighed. "Right."

If only Little Spoon was real instead of made up by Vera, Little Spoon could save her somehow.

Then and there, just like that, Vera had an idea. It might not be a good idea. It might be the most terrible idea in the history of the world. But it was all she had.

☆ ☆ ☆

That evening Vera's mother tried a new recipe—chicken cooked with a rice-shaped pasta called orzo, simmered together with chicken broth, lemons, and Kalamata olives. The chicken-orzo-lemon-olive dish turned out to be delicious.

"Yum!" Vera said, when she had eaten every bite.

Her mother gave a happy laugh. "I know!" she agreed. "And it was ridiculously easy, too."

Vera practiced piano extra-long just because the Mozart sonata she was learning was so beautiful she wanted to make every note of it beautiful, too.

"That piece is coming along so nicely," Vera's mother told her as they climbed into Vera's bed for the next chapters of *A Wrinkle in Time*. Vera felt herself glowing from her mother's praise, even if her mother was never going to sound proud and happy like that about making a comic.

When they finished the chapter where Meg rescues her missing father from imprisonment in a transparent column and rushes into his protective arms, Vera's throat had a lump in it so big she could hardly swallow.

"I wish . . ." she began. She wanted to say, *I*

wish my father could come back, but the words couldn't get past the lump blocking them.

"I know," her mother said softly. "I still miss him every single day. And then every single day I'm so grateful I have you."

Vera snuggled closer to her mother.

If Nixie had been there, Nixie would have poked Vera, and the poke would have meant, *Ask her again about comic-con! Ask her right now!* But the moment was too special and perfect for Vera to ask for anything more.

After her mother had tucked her in, however, Vera turned the light back on and slipped her Little Spoon comic out from beneath her pillow. Little Spoon had already rescued everyone in the spoon drawer from the snooty lady who was going to throw the spoons away and get newer, shinier, fancier ones.

While the other spoons were asleep, Little Spoon, Plastic Spoon, and Chopsticks had polished the rest of the spoons, even Big Spoon, with special polish Little Spoon had made from a secret formula; then Plastic Spoon and Chopsticks polished Little Spoon, too. The next morning the spoons looked so dazzlingly

bright and gleamingly shiny that Lady Snob-barella had said, "Oh, you beautiful spoons! How could I ever have thought of getting rid of you! I'm going to keep you forever!" And Big Spoon said, "Little Spoon, I'm so proud of you!"

Now there was going to be a great big celebration of all the spoons in all the drawers in all the houses in the whole neighborhood. It was called Spoonic-Con. Every single spoon was going to Spoonic-Con, except for one.

Big Spoon had said Little Spoon couldn't go. Big Spoon said Spoonic-Con would be too crowded, too noisy, too confusing. She said there would be a lot of very weird spoons there, spoons covered with crazy designs and strange pictures. She said Spoonic-Con would be too overwhelming for a spoon as small as Little Spoon.

Vera worked hard on the final picture of Little Spoon alone in the empty silverware drawer, abandoned by the other spoons who had raced merrily off to Spoonic-Con, forgetting all about her. Tears dripped down Little

Spoon's face, leaving spots of rust where they fell onto her handle.

It was the saddest picture Vera had ever drawn.

She slipped out of bed, glad her mother's bedroom door was already closed, and tiptoed down the stairs. She left *The Secret Life of Little Spoon* on the kitchen counter next to the coffeemaker where her mother made her first cup of coffee every morning without fail. Then she crept back up to bed again.

What if her mother didn't bother to read it and, mildly annoyed at finding school stuff where it wasn't supposed to be, just tucked it into Vera's backpack?

If she did start to read it, what if she flipped through the first few pages and didn't get all the way to the end?

If she did get all the way to the end, what if it hurt her feelings, the way James's comic had hurt Nolan and Boogie?

Or . . . would it . . . could it . . . make her change her mind?

★ ten ★

The next morning, at seven o'clock, Vera's mother poked her head into Vera's room to see if she was awake, the way she always did on school days. "Rise and shine!" she said in the partly cheery, partly stressed voice she had on busy mornings.

Had she seen *Little Spoon* on the counter?

Had she read it?

Or not?

As soon as Vera came into the kitchen for breakfast, dressed and ready for school, she couldn't keep her eyes from straying to the counter by the coffeemaker. The pile of drawings had disappeared.

"It's in your backpack," Vera's mother said briskly. "I figured you'd need it for camp."

Vera thought her mother's lips quivered as she turned to the stove to dish up the scrambled eggs onto two plates. Was her mother hurt? Or angry? Or both? She certainly wasn't handing Vera a signed permission form for comic-con to tuck in her backpack next to her comic.

"Have a good day," her mother told her, as she pulled up in front of the elementary school to drop Vera off. She leaned over to give Vera a kiss the same way she always did.

"Bye," Vera said. She imagined her voice coming out in tiny lettering inside a tiny speech bubble.

So that was that.

☆ ☆ ☆

At school, one look at Vera's unsmiling face must have let Nixie know Vera's mother hadn't changed her mind. At lunch, Nixie clearly did her best to avoid any mention of camp, comics, or comic-con, letting the other girls at the table talk about their favorite cat videos instead.

"We can go bowling again this weekend if you want," Nixie said in a rush, as she and Vera headed outside for lunch recess, trailing behind the others. Nixie might as well have added, *So you'll have at least* something *to look forward to since you can't go to comic-con.*

"Thanks," Vera said politely. "That would be nice."

"Are you sure it wouldn't help if—" Nixie began.

Vera cut her off. "I'm sure."

At camp Brian and Buzz-Bee spent the first half hour whipping everyone else into a frenzy of excitement about comic-con. Why had Vera even bothered to come to camp today, if she was the only one left out of everything? Of course, with her mother at her office working, there was nowhere else for her to go. She was relieved when Colleen beckoned her over to help staple a big stack of pamphlets for some future after-school programs. At least Colleen seemed to understand how Vera felt.

Finally Brian said, "Okay! I can tell everyone's too wound up to do any real work this afternoon, so . . . movie time!"

The campers gathered in the storytelling area, and *Superman* began to play. Great. When Vera's mother came to pick her up, she'd find everyone staring at the movie projected onto the wall, looking "slack jawed and vacant eyed," as she liked to say, the final proof that comics camp and all comics everywhere were a great big waste of time and money.

Sure enough, when Vera's mom slipped into the room an hour later, most of the campers were sprawled on the floor in just the kind of sloppy posture her mother hated most. Vera glanced at the clock on the wall. Her mother was early.

Good-bye forever, comics camp.

Slowly Vera got up to leave. Her mother was already deep in conversation with Colleen. Then Buzz-Bee went over to join them.

Vera allowed herself one last desperate stab of hope. Maybe Buzz-Bee *could* convince her mother? Vera held back, just in case, hardly daring to let herself breathe.

Now Colleen was digging through her thick camp folder and pulling out a piece of paper to hand to Vera's mother.

Now Vera's mother was writing something on it.

Vera couldn't make herself wait any longer. As she approached the three of them, her mother met her eyes. She gave Vera one small nod, followed by a tremulous smile. Then Vera flung her arms around her mother's waist and held on tight.

"Can I really go to comic-con?" she asked. "Can I really truly go?"

Her mother's eyes glistened with what looked like tears.

"Yes, Little Spoon," her mother said softly. "Big Spoon has had all day to think about a lot of things. So yes, you may really truly go."

☆ ☆ ☆

Comic-con was everything Vera's mother had said it would be.

It was crowded.

It was noisy.

It was overwhelming.

Most of all, it was wonderful.

Brian and Buzz-Bee would have let the campers wander around by themselves. "Wander! Explore! Let it wash over you like a tidal wave!" Brian had said. But Colleen made rules that everybody had to have a buddy (Vera had Nixie, of course), and they had to stay in sight of an adult, either a teacher or one of the parents. Vera knew her mother would never take off work for a comic-con. She was just happy her mother had let her come after all.

Harper looked regal in her princess dress, complete with tiara, long white gloves, and a sweeping train Boogie kept tripping over. Boogie's tiny Superman cape looked so funny on him, Vera and Nixie couldn't stop giggling. Even Nolan was speechless, with not a single fact to offer, and James looked more excited this afternoon than on all the other afternoons of camp put together.

At every booth, artists sat sketching, drawing, painting, working on comics and graphic novels right there before Vera's eyes, despite the hordes of wildly costumed people surging by. It was as if nothing in the world mattered to them except to sit with pencils, pens, and paintbrushes and make characters come alive.

Vera understood completely.

Brian finally found the room where kids' comics were on display, mounted on large free-standing bulletin boards flanking every wall. Where was Little Spoon? Vera hoped she was on the same bulletin board with Mistress Bow-Wow, and the flying toast, Princess Esmerelda, and Backwards Benny. Comic-con suddenly did seem like a huge and terrifying place for one little spoon to be.

Then she saw it, the one-page entry from her comic book, with the shock of seeing something so familiar in such an unfamiliar place.

A blue ribbon hanging next to it said SPECIAL MERIT.

None of the other comics—and hers *was* with the other After-School Superstars—had a blue ribbon, not even Harper's. Just *Little Spoon, drawn by Vera Vance, age eight.*

"Look!" Nixie squealed. "You got a ribbon, Vera! Everybody, Vera got a ribbon!"

Buzz-Bee put her arm around Vera's shoulders and gave her a squeeze. Then the others— Nolan, Boogie, even James and Harper—were saying *"Congratulations!"* and *"Good job!"* and *"Woo-hoo!"*

Vera felt a pang of pity for Harper, who had been so sure her comic was the best.

Should she say something to her?

Saying something wasn't as hard as it used to be.

"I thought yours was better than mine," Vera told Harper, as the others started looking at more of the kids' comics on display. She had to raise her voice to be heard above the din. "Honestly, I did."

Harper brushed back her hair with a princess-gloved hand. "My mom's going to freak out, but I don't care. She's the one who's into comics, not me."

Vera stared at her. "My mom's the opposite! She hates comics! Well, she used to hate them."

"My mom drew part of mine," Harper confessed. "She kept fixing up my drawings every night after I brought them home, like nothing I ever did was good enough." Harper paused. "I'm Little Spoon, and my mom's Big Spoon. It's like you based your comic on my mom and me, the way James based his on Nolan and Boogie, except you don't even know my mom, and your comic wasn't mean like his. It was just—I don't know—*true*."

That was what Brian had said about comics back in the first week: because comic-book characters were simple, drawn with so few features, it was easy for everyone all over the world to see themselves in them.

Vera had a strange thought. This whole past month, she had been on her own hero's journey. Signing up for comics camp was her call to adventure. Buzz-Bee and Brian were her mentors, and Nixie, Nolan, and Boogie—even, in their own way, James and Harper—had been her helpers. Convincing her mother to let her go to comic-con had been her supreme ordeal. It had all happened just the way a comic-book version of the hero's journey was supposed to.

Before she could think about this any more, Boogie was asking when it was time to eat, and someone else had to go to the bathroom, and the group started to head off for other comic-con adventures.

Vera gave one more glance at Little Spoon, with the bright blue ribbon hanging beside her. Then, in the doorway, she saw her mom, peering into the room with an anxious, uncomfortable gaze.

She had come.

She was there.

Nixie seized Vera's hand and pulled her toward the door. Then, with her other hand, she grabbed hold of Vera's mother and led them both back to the display wall.

"Vera got a ribbon!" Nixie squealed, using her head to point at Little Spoon. "A special ribbon for being the best comics maker ever! See?"

"Oh, honey!" Her mother gathered Vera into a hug, acting just as proud as when Vera had won the piano prize last year.

"Hooray for Little Spoon!" Nixie shouted.

Her mother gave Vera another hug as she added in a whisper, "And hooray for you!"

Claudia Mills wrote her first book at age six. The title was *My Book*, and it was filled with "nacher pictures" of "the rainbow," "the sky," and "the trees." It was never published, but since then she has produced more than sixty published titles, including picture books, easy readers, chapter books, novels for middle-schoolers, and even academic books for grown-ups.

In addition to writing books, she has been a college professor, both in the philosophy department at the University of Colorado at Boulder and in the graduate program in children's literature at Hollins University in Roanoke.

Her books have been named Notable Books of the Year by the American Library Association and translated into French, Spanish, Italian, Hebrew, Japanese, Korean, and Chinese. All of her books were written between five and seven in the morning, lying on the couch with her favorite clipboard, narrow-ruled pad of white paper, and fine-tipped black marker pens, while drinking hot chocolate.

Grace Zong has illustrated many books for children, including *Goldy Luck and the Three Pandas* by Natasha Yim and *Mrs. McBee Leaves Room 3* by Gretchen Brandenburg McLellan. She divides her time between South Korea and New York.